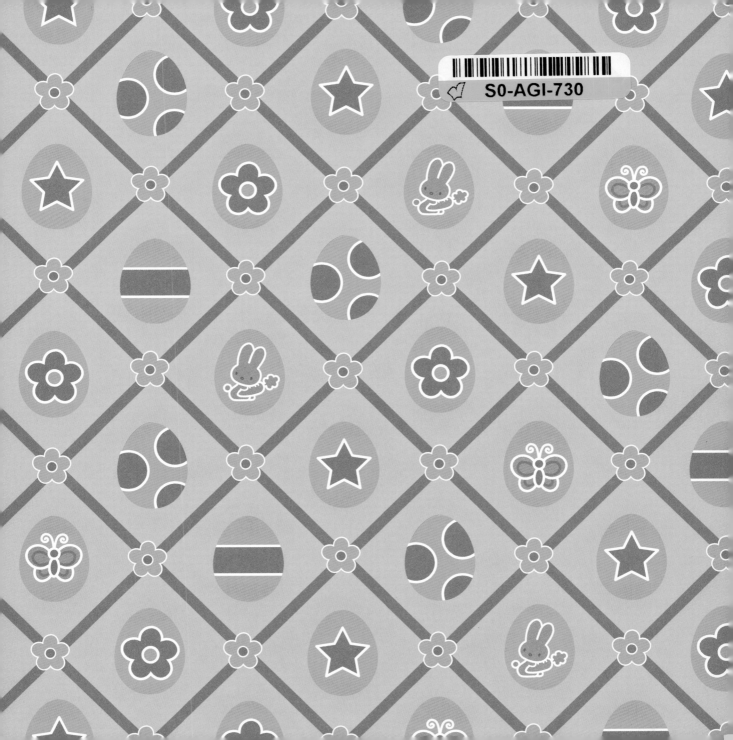

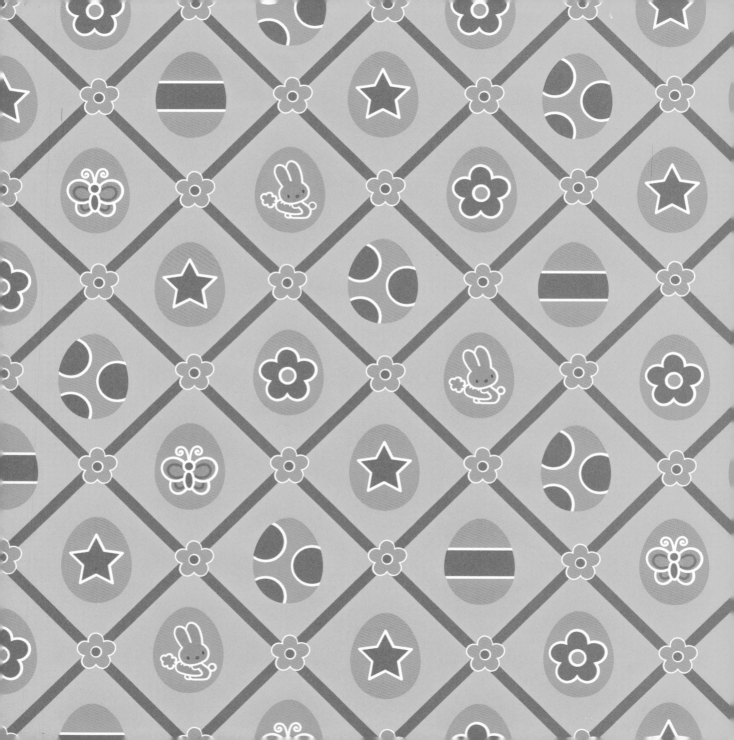

Hello Kitty's

Easter Bonnet Surprise

Hello Kitty's
Easter Bonnet Surprise

LuLu's Hat Shop

illustrated by Jean Hirashima

HARRY N. ABRAMS, INC., PUBLISHERS

"Oh, no!" said Hello Kitty. "How could I have lost it?"

"Lost what?" asked her sister Mimmy.
"My Easter bonnet!" said Hello Kitty.

"I thought it was in my room," she said, "but I can't find it anywhere."

"It was such a pretty bonnet," said Mimmy, "just perfect for the Easter parade."

"I must have left it somewhere," said Hello Kitty. "If I go back to all the places I went yesterday, maybe I will find it."

"Let's look in my room first," said Mimmy. But the bonnet was not in Mimmy's room.

As they left their house, Hello Kitty and Mimmy ran into their friend Kathy. They explained the problem to her.

"I know," said Kathy, "maybe you left it at school."

But the bonnet was not in their classroom, on the playground, or anywhere else they looked.

"Could you have left it on the bus?" asked Mimmy.

But the bonnet was not at the bus company's lost and found either.

Hello Kitty was getting more and more worried. She asked her friends Thomas, Rory, Fifi, and Joey, because she had stopped by each their houses yesterday on her way home from school. But none of them had seen the Easter bonnet either.

Finally, Hello Kitty went to her grandparents' house, where Grandpa White was working in his garden.

"Grandpa White," she said sadly, "I can't find my Easter bonnet anywhere, and I've looked for it everywhere."

Exhausted, she plopped down under a tree, next to a banged-up old basket.

"Hmmm," she said to herself as she turned the basket over, "I think I have an idea!"

She asked her friends to help her gather flowers and other pretty things. Then, they worked and worked, for hours and hours...

And the next day...

Hello Kitty had the biggest and most beautiful bonnet in the whole Easter parade!

"Do you know what?" she said to Mimmy. "I don't care if I never find my old hat. This one we all made together is just perfect!"

Illustrations by Jean Hirashima
Designed by Celina Carvalho

Library of Congress Cataloging-in-Publication Data

Hello Kitty's Easter bonnet surprise / illustrations by Jean Hirashima.
p. cm.
Summary: When Hello Kitty loses her new Easter bonnet before the big
parade, Grandma White's old wicker basket provides a solution.
ISBN 0-8109-4819-2
[1. Hats—Fiction. 2. Easter—Fiction. 3. Lost and found
possessions—Fiction. 4. Cats—Fiction.] I. Title: Easter bonnet
surprise. II. Hirashima, Jean, ill.

PZ7.H3744534 2004
[E]—dc22
2003022142ISBN 0-8109-4819-2

Printed and bound in the United States
10 9 8 7 6 5 4 3 2 1

Harry N. Abrams, Inc.
100 Fifth Avenue
New York, NY 10011
www.abramsbooks.com

Abrams is a subsidiary of
LA MARTINIÈRE
G R O U P E